This book belongs to

_____

Ninja Life Hacks™

This book is dedicated to my children - Mikey, Kobe, and Jojo.
Life is what happens when you're looking at your smartphone.

Unplugged Ninja

Pictures by
Jelena Stupar

By Mary Nhin

To be calm and cool, I make a choice to stay mindful.

For example, when I feel compelled to be on my electronics every other minute, I reset my habits by doing something active or creative.

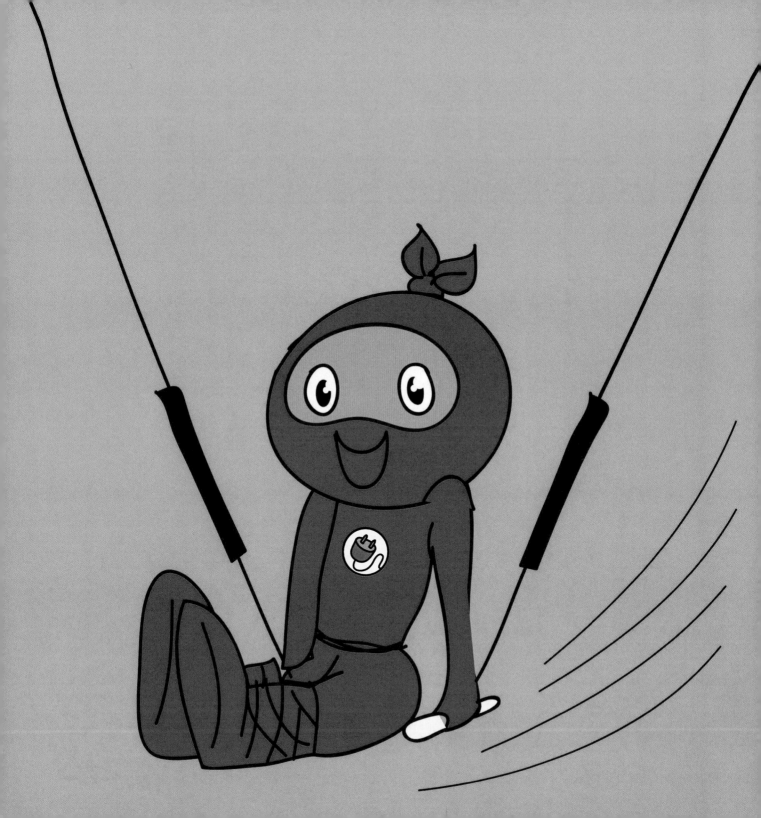

When I'm feeling irritable or angry, I reconnect with nature by biking, playing a sport, or fishing.

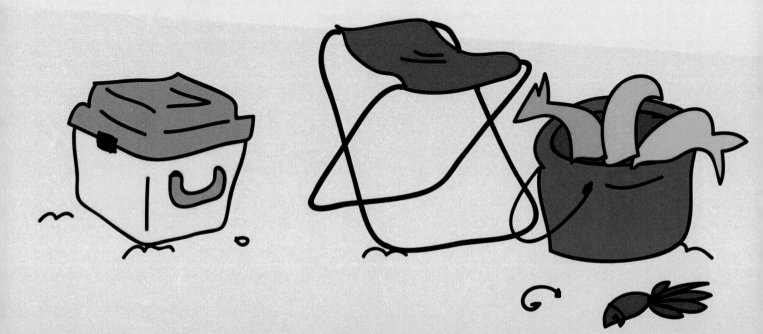

And if I'm feeling anxious or stressed out, I relax by reading or spending quiet time alone.

But I haven't always known how to be calm and collected...

When I couldn't find my electronics, I would begin to panic.

If the wifi suddenly stopped working, I would get upset.

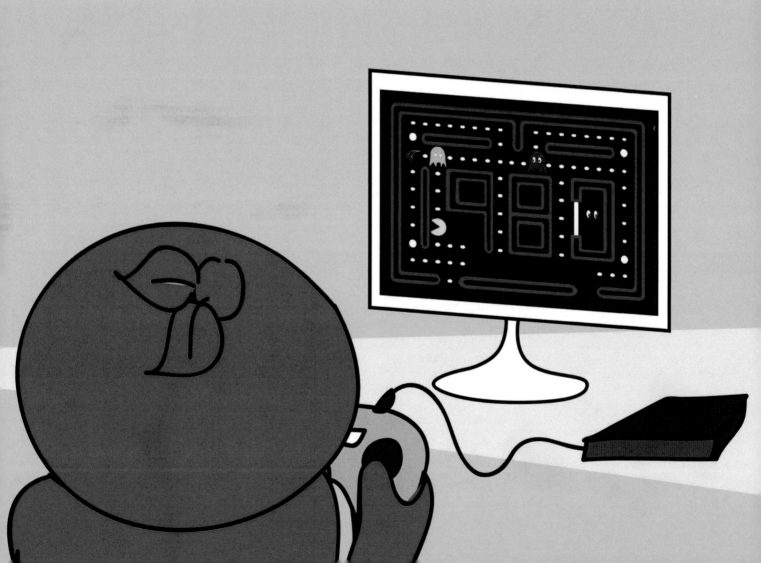

And if I spent a lot of time on electronics, I would become irritable.

But all of that changed one day when Kind Ninja suggested I try a fun, new way to go about my day.

"Do you want me to show you?" Kind Ninja asked.

Reset by doing a fun activity. It can be something active or creative.

Next, reconnect with nature by going outside.

Then, relax with music, a book, or a bath.

The next day, I woke up remembering what Kind Ninja said about the 3 Rs.

After breakfast, I decided to practice the 1st R, reset.

I created a new game with my dog.

To practice the 2nd R, reconnect, I went outside to play.

I was having so much fun, I didn't even realize how late it had gotten.

Before I knew it, I was performing Kind Ninja's 3rd R by relaxing in a long, warm bath.

It had been a spectacular day. And as I drifted off to sleep, I thought to myself...

If you're ever feeling like you might need a digital detox, remembering the 3 Rs could be your secret weapon against screen addiction.

RESET.
RECONNECT.
RELAX.

Download your Unplugged Ninja Lesson Plan at NinjaLifeHacks.tv

@marynhin   @GrowGrit
#NinjaLifeHacks

Mary Nhin   Ninja Life Hacks

Ninja Life Hacks

Made in the USA
Las Vegas, NV
11 October 2021